Kamal's Quest

By
Cynthia Profilet

Illustrated by
Francis Livingston

Sterling Press, Inc.
Jackson, Mississippi

Kamal's Quest © 1993
by Cynthia Cain Profilet

Library of Congress
Catalog Card Number: 93-93581

ISBN 0-9637735-0-X

Published by
Sterling Press, Inc.
Jackson, Mississippi

Illustrated by
Francis Livingston
San Anselmo, California

Design by
William Dunn Design
Santa Clara, California

Printed in the United States of America.

To
Abdulaziz Mubarak Al-Khalifa

Thank you for the hospitality
shown me while I lived in Bahrain.
Your inspiration and encouragement
have made this story come alive.

~ Cynthia Profilet

The coffee pot is a symbol of hospitality in Bahrain.

Author's Note

This story is about a country and a camel. Bahrain is a tiny island in the Arabian Gulf. Kamal is a camel.

Little is known about the unique character of both this country and the camel.

It is my hope that all who read <u>Kamal's Quest</u> will develop a greater appreciation of these gentle, warm-hearted people in this mysterious land, and will grow to love the camel as I do.

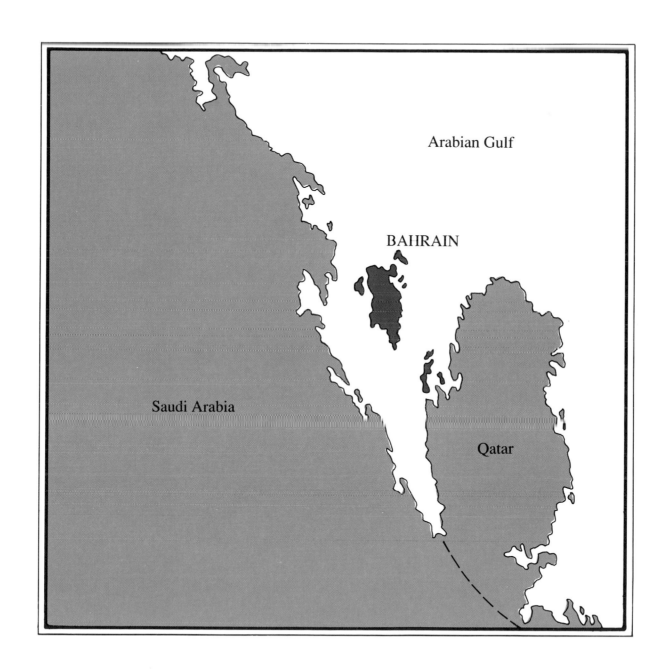

Arabian Gulf

BAHRAIN

Saudi Arabia

Qatar

The Camel

The sun scorched the Arabian desert sand. Fiery bits of dust charged the air. The temperature had soared to one hundred eighteen degrees today on Bahrain, the small desert island in the Arabian Gulf.

Exhausted from their struggle with the heat, the baby camel, Kamal, and his mother rested under the cooling shade of a palm tree. Kamal nestled against his mother's soft, furry side. He was still a young calf, and he was his mother's pride and joy.

This morning mother and baby were making a trip to the *suq,* the market place. Two young boys lifted Kamal into a net on the hump of another camel. His mother followed closely behind. As with all mother camels, she must have her baby in sight at all times.

At last the camel caravan began to move slowly...slowly...nearer to the suq.

Ten camels, roped tail to nose, made soft, squishy sounds in the heavy sand. Small boys and men walked beside them prodding them on with sticks.

As the line of camels neared the suq, a wonderland of new sights, sounds, and smells flooded the young camel's senses. At first, Kamal was afraid, yet excited!

Traveling along the narrow, sandy road, they were surrounded by a brilliant array of colors. In the background, they could hear rumblings of street vendors and shoppers begging for bargains. Mystical sounds of Arabian music seemed to slither through the air like smoke, only to return with a hard, driving beat. "TWANG - TWANG! ta - ta! TWANG! TWANG! TWANG!" The camels' pace picked up a beat in response to the rhythmic songs. They adored the music of their native land.

Strong smells hung in the air—meat, bread, oil, and vegetables. These combined to make a unique scent.

Kamal sniffed and held his head high as he rode along. He didn't want to miss anything.

At the end of the day, it was time to return to their village. Home seemed far away, and they felt the weight of the day in their feet. The camels could move only about one mile per hour. It was time for a rest.

A young boy lifted Kamal from his net. He and his mother settled down under the shadows of a palm tree.

These moments alone with his mother were the happiest times Kamal could remember.

CRACK! A whip snapped! Wild screams! A band of theives came from nowhere! Six men tore through the resting caravan and stole everything they had bought at the suq. These wild strangers also took two of the finest camels with them. Suddenly, Kamal's mother was gone—in an instant, gone forever!

Shocked! Terrified! Kamal moaned and groaned. His mother had been taken away from him. His eyes filled with sorrow, and he shuddered with sadness. Faith and hope were gone.

Kamal's hurt and fear turned into anger. He spit and stomped. In rage, he squealed! No one would ever get close to him again. His heart grew cold and hard.

Time passed. Ahmed, his owner, had quickly discovered that Kamal had a gift for running. It was his birthright. He was a *Dromedary*—a camel with one hump instead of two. He was built to run at top speed.

"Kamal, you will be the finest racing camel on Bahrain," Ahmed promised.

"First, I must train you. You will travel faster than a shooting star soaring across the moonlit sky. Honor and praise will come to you."

Ahmed carefully groomed Kamal for his first race. He taught him to trot, to canter, and to gallop. Ahmed gave Kamal the very best training. Soon it would be time to show Kamal's great speed to others.

After long hours of hard work, Kamal and Ahmed were tired. The radiant sun shone down upon their heads. Trickles of water streamed down their faces. Relief was not far away. Ahmed gazed at the beautiful sight in front of him. It was the Mosque, the Holy Place of worship for Muslims. In this quiet, cool chamber, he knew he would find rest.

"Come, Kamal. Let us go to the Mosque. I will find a cool place for you to wait."

As he entered the Holy Place, Ahmed removed his shoes and knelt on the thick carpet. Facing Mecca, the Holy City, he uttered his prayers in humble tones. Ahmed was troubled by his camel's restless spirit. He asked Allah, his god, to give him the strength and wisdom to lead Kamal. Ahmed felt that Allah understood.

The Race

Excitement filled the air. Kamal and the other young camels were making their final preparations for the race. Small humps bobbled up and down, and knobby knees wobbled in all directions.

POW! The sweltering stillness was shattered by a gun shot, and the race began. Kamal lunged through the choking dust, leaving the other camels behind. He ran close to the ground. His lower lip hung wide open as he rolled back and forth along the course.

Suddenly a larger, darker camel came from behind.

CLOP! CLOP! The pounding boomed in Kamal's ears.

The fire of his opponent's breath singed his tender skin.

Back and forth, they fought for the lead. They were nose to nose.

Kamal lowered his head and raised his ears.

Buried deep within him, the will to win rose up with a mighty force. GASPING— he lunged toward the finish line.

At last—

HE HAD WON THE RACE!

A *sheik,* a member of the royal family, was standing close to the finish line. A warm smile illuminated his face as his gentle eyes fell on Kamal. The beauty and grace of the small camel captured his heart.

He sent his servants to Kamal. They brushed and groomed him. They fed him only the best dates, grain, and green fodder, and dressed him in ornamental cloth with red and gold tassels. Tiny brass bells were hung from his head gear. The sheik gave Kamal a splendidly decorated saddle of the finest leather.

Yet, Kamal was still filled with bitterness, and no amount of kindness and generosity could warm his cold heart. He cared for neither man nor beast. He wanted his mother.

Kamal continued his training sessions with Ahmed, but he remained frustrated. A powerful urge to rebel surged through him. Gradually, this feeling controlled him, and he lashed out at Ahmed. Kamal bit his owner as he vented his rage. Turning away, he deserted Ahmed and headed for the desert. Maybe he would find his mother...

He continued to wander through the desert. The stifling heat and the constant stirring of the sandstorm forced Kamal to continue his quest. At night, Kamal would gaze up at the full moon. All was silent.

Not a soul was in sight. Life was empty.

One day while trudging through the sand, he thought he heard a voice. It was a very weak, distant groan..."Help! Help! Help me...water...water...water."

Slowly, Kamal walked toward the feeble cries. A gust of wind pushed him closer to the weak pleas for help.

The ragged, dirty stranger was writhing and crawling on the ground. He pointed feebly to his parched, dry mouth and croaked again, "Water! Water!"

Kamal turned away, but the pitiful cries made him pause. The old poison bubbled within him. "Why should I help him?" The urge to kick and spit on the man was strong.

Suddenly, he stopped. Something beneath the layers of bitterness in the animal stirred. There was a familiar sadness in the man's eyes. Kamal understood. This man needed him. "I will help him," Kamal thought. For the first time since his mother had been taken from him, Kamal wanted to help another, to give of himself.

With noisy snorting and clumsy movements, Kamal bent his front legs and dropped to his knees. He folded his hind legs and fell to the ground beside the man. Pitting his elbows into the sand, the man struggled, edging closer to the camel. Slowly, he stretched his arms upward, and pulling the full weight of his body, he mounted the camel. Kamal trembled as he straightened his legs with an awkward jerk and rose to his feet.

The Oasis

This man needed water immediately to live, but the man's weight was a great burden for the young camel. The special gift of all camels is their ability to find water. Kamal's acute sense of smell led them to an oasis. Beneath the cooling shade of the palm trees, a small pond awaited them. The man slid into the water, taking huge gulps. Kamal watched as the man began to regain strength.

The stranger rinsed his face and neck and washed the gritty sand from his hair. Finally, he paused, looked up at Kamal, and smiled. This smile again kindled a warm glow in the heart of the camel.

In deep, gentle tones, the man spoke to Kamal. He moved his arms in the direction of the suq. Kamal's heart ruled his actions now. He knew that he could take him to the suq.

Kamal led the way as the man walked by his side. The man spoke warmly and softly to the camel. He patted him on his side and sang to him. The music was different, but it soothed and charmed Kamal. Memories of his mother filled his heart.

As they arrived at the suq, the man entered a tiny shop in a nearby alley. He was out of Kamal's sight for quite a while. Kamal struggled impatiently as he waited for him. He must not lose this man. Although he tried to be very brave, Kamal could not hide his doubt. "What if he does not return?" Kamal thought, "I will be lonely again." Fear raced through his mind.

Finally, the man returned with a broad smile on his lips. Gently stroking Kamal's face, he whispered to the anxious beast, "You were there when I needed a friend. You saved my life. I would like for you to spend the rest of your life in my care."

Kamal could not understand the words, but the meaning was clear to the camel.

The friendship of this man would give value and meaning to his life. Peace ruled in Kamal's heart on this tiny island of Bahrain. The spirits of five thousand years seemed to rise up and say,

"Love, Peace, and Joy will remain on this island forever."

Glossary

Dromedary (drom′ ĭ - der ē) — a camel with only one hump.

Mosque (môsk) — the Muslim place of worship.

Sheik (shāk) — a title given to male members of the ruling family.

Suq (sook) — an old market area of a Middle Eastern city.